# The Road That Never Ends

Jayani Mattu

 pencil

ISBN 978-93-5667-183-6
© Jayani Mattu 2022
Published in India 2022 by Pencil

*A brand of*

One Point Six Technologies Pvt. Ltd.
123, Building J2, Shram Seva Premises,
Wadala Truck Terminal, Wadala (E)
Mumbai 400037, Maharashtra, INDIA
**E** connect@thepencilapp.com
**W** www.thepencilapp.com



DISCLAIMER: *This is a work of fiction. Names, characters, places, events and incidents are the products of the author's imagination. The opinions expressed in this book do not seek to reflect the views of the Publisher.*

# Author biography

Warm Greetings Dear Readers!

I am Jayani. I am a young girl from school. I am a Libra born on 29 September, 2009. I have won prizes in chess, public speaking, singing, academics etc. I love music and art and crafts. I play 3 musical instruments and I can speak 5 languages. I am an avid follower of soccer. I love biographies as they are intresting as well as knowledgable. I also like reading encyclopaedias. I want to thank you all for spending your precious time reading my books. I would love to hear feedback from you!

You all can send me on my gmail-jayanimattu2009@gmail.com

THANK YOU!

# CONTENTS

# Acknowledgements

Greetings to all the readers! here, I present my third book ' The Road That Never Ends' which is horror and I thought that after writing adventure; let me add some horror to my collection. As I always say and believe that ' in the making of a brilliant mind, many people make efforts to make someone's dream come true. I also have got many blessings and have seen the efforts made by my parents, family and my teachers. I am so happy to recive the best companions in the race of making my future cheerful and bright. My friends with whom I have fun in school, My techers who make me more brighter everyday and my parents and family who keep encouraging me and helping me in my daily needs. Well, How much thank you I'll say it is less as compared to the efforts they have done for me. A big Thank You! to all who make my life feel like life and love me the most!
THANK YOU!

# Chapter 1

The morning was heartening but a bit sad as my family was ready to leave our home and shift to a new one. It was my father's transfer to a city. I don't know much about, but I do know that it was Newbrook that we were shifting to; was a few miles away.

I was in my room. Daisy was in my hands. She's my favorite person. My dog. My posters of football, cartoons and photos of me, mom, dad and daisy were not there. they were in the carton that's in the pickups truck.

"Honey come down we have to go now," said my mom.

"coming mom"

I touched the walls of my room to feel the feeling of amazement and my memories with it. I remember well how I used to play in the room when I was little. Well, I'm little now also just 12. But was talking about when I was little then 12.

"Oh! Sorry I forgot to introduce myself. My name is........

"Jim! Will you come fast?! Or we leave without you!?"

"Oh! Boy today I'm surely going to be scolded! Better be invisible in a jiffy!"

"see mom, here I am. On time!"

Daisy was at my back. I took her and sat in the car. The pickups truck had already left. I could hear it's rumbling clearly.

The time came to bid a farewell to my home, my friends, my neighbors and everyone. I am going to miss them a lot. Our family settled in the car and it went up to the destination. I could see my home back from the car's window. The time felt like; it's moving really fast.

I had a strange feeling. My mouth was shut and the mind was like lost in something though I wasn't thinking anything.

I was just, looking out of the window. I don't remember what I was looking at.

Suddenly! Something jumped on me really fast!

I shouted aahhh!

"Oh! It's you Daisy. You nearly gave me a heart attack!"

"Jim, hold on tight! The road's going to be a little bumpy," said father

"got it! doing as you say sir!" I exclaimed.

Suddenly, the clouds filled with darkness.

"probably it's going to rain soon," said mother

"yeah, sure it's look like it will come soon" father said.

I opened the car window. The darkness was suffocating me. I put my head out. We were travelling on a bridge probably in a forest. Then, I saw that it was a hurricane at the side!

"DAD! STOP! It's a hurricane there!"

Dad tried for the brakes but it fail!

Suddenly the road beneath us broke into pieces! And we fell down the cliff!

# Chapter 2

Oh! I got a shock suddenly! Daisy was licking me. I looked out of the window it was sunny!

"honey are you alright? You look a bit tensed" mom asked

"yes mom, I'm fine just had a terrible dream. Have we arrived in Newbrook?"

"yes son! We have. see, that is our new home!" dad yelled.

Oh! Boy the new home was much bigger and spacious than our old one. Our neighborhood was also really advanced. I got a shrill cry of excitement as we went in.

The pickups truck was already there waiting for us. As we arrived at our home it upholded all our things in.

I and daisy ran into our new garden which was delightful! I took the Frisby and she and I started to play. I gave her the pup treats. Oh! They are finished.

"mom can I go to buy daisy's pup treats when we finish upholding our stuff?"

"yes! But only when someone adult will go with you. You don't know the city well you can get lost"

"okay mom. Can I take Jack uncle with me?"

"yes. He lives in our neighborhood. I will call him then you can go"

"okay mom. As you say"

Jack uncle was my favorite uncle. I love to play with him. I am glad he lives here only! Meanwhile, mom's calling uncle Jack, I can give my room a makeover!

"come on Daisy! Let's get ready"

I and Daisy went upstairs in our new room. First, we cleaned everything there. then I took the carton on which 'Jim's stuff' was written. Then, we took out the things and started getting ready.

The room was painted just like I wanted. Space! I am interested in space. It so big and nice! Then I settled everything. My posters, photos on the wall and books on the bookshelf. In another carton on which' daisy's stuff' was written; I set all her things at a corner in my room.

And finally, the moment I've been waiting for! UNCLE JACK ARRIVED! I saw him entering at the gate from my window. I ran as fast as I can.

# Chapter 3

"Uncle Jack! I am glad to see you!"

"Me too Jim! Look, how big you have been since last year I met you!"

I gave Uncle Jack a big hug and showed him my room.

"Jim let Uncle Jack have some tea first. He isn't going anywhere!" mom said.

"okay mom. Uncle Jack you have your tea fast then we will go for a stroll!"

"okay dear, But first let me have my tea"

As soon as Uncle Jack finished his tea we went for the stroll. In between Uncle Jack and I had many talks. He showed me all the neighborhood. This was the best day of my life! I went to Uncle's house and had some tea. When we were heading to my home. A girl of about my age stopped us.

Hello! Uncle Jack! She said. She looked at me for a while and left.

"uncle, you know her?"

 "yes, Jim. She lives in the next home of yours. She is a very nice girl."

When we arrived home, I saw the same girl at the next door. She smiled at me and waved at me. I waved back.

I haven't got any friends since I left my previous home. Probably, she could be my friend?

Now the time came for uncle Jack to leave.

"Uncle can't you stay any longer?"

"I hope I could Jim. But I have to go."

"okay uncle. Bye!"

I went up to my room and looked out of the window. Daisy came towards me I hold her in my arms and we looked outside together. The girl was combing her hair.

"hi" I said stammering.

"hi" she said.

"today's weather really nice, isn't it?"

"yes, I haven't seen you here earlier are you new?" she said

"yes, I am. Uh, would you- would you like to play outside?"

"sure. Just give me a minute" she said.

"okay" I replied.

I told mom that I was going to play with her. As I walked out of the door, she was already outside waiting for me. Then after the greetings we went to play in my garden with Daisy. She is surely a very nice girl as uncle said. I liked playing with her. Her name is Della.

We didn't looked at the time. Oh! Its evening. "bye Della! see you tomorrow."

With this we went our homes. I am glad I found a new friend. Now, tomorrow would be a new start, I am going to school! Yes well, it's kind of fun but still as I have stayed home for many days because of shifting I don't want to go to school. But I have to, oh, life's so difficult! Couldn't it be so easy?!

Well, okay! Sometimes we have to adjust, right?! okay good night! everyone I got to get ready for tomorrow.

# Chapter 4

so new start, new day, new morning I can't say much! So, Daisy was in my bed sleeping with me. Mom came to wake me up.

"Jim, you don't want to get late for your first day of school?"

"yes mom, just I don't want to go"

"but, why? Jim, don't you like your new school"

"no! it's just….

"I understand. It's difficult for you to adjust to the new surroundings. But you can't stay at home forever! Don't worry you'll adjust it takes time. It's taking time for me too! Don't worry, okay?"

Mom kissed and hugged me. Now I feel a bit okay! Okay fine now let's get ready!

"let's turn some music on!"

Music's my life one thing I tell you! I like it very much. It's just miraculous! Okay with some beats on I started getting ready. Then, daisy oh! I'm going to miss her. She's not letting me go.

"daisy I'll come back as fast as I can!"

"Jim, you know who's going to pick you up?"

"you mom, of course"

"no! it's ……. Uncle Jack!"

"oh! What's a nice morning! Best day!"

I stood of my bed and rushed and rushed just to get ready before Uncle Jack arrives! I was doing everything fast. Brushing, bathing, dressing, eating and every other thing.

Then, I got ready to early that Uncle Jack hasn't arrived yet. I looked at the watch it was 6 AM when mom waked me and now it's just 6:10! The school's going to start at 7:15 what am I going to do now? it's so boring waiting 1 hour!

Fine! Daisy come we are going for a walk!

Daisy came running and we went out the street for a walk. Oh! Though I have to wait for 1 hour till Uncle Jack arrives let me spend this 1 hour the best 1 hour of my life! How good ideas I make!

Daisy and I jumping and danced like the drops of rain sizzling in the cheerful morning. Up and down the streets we talked and laughed the way while seeing a beautiful view of small animals strolling with us all around. butterflies in the garden, squirrels up the trees, and much more.

As I kept walking, I thought that Della would have been ready for her school by now too. Let me go and meet her.

I went back on my way home to see her next door. I rang the bell and her mother came outside to accompany me.

"Who are you, sweetheart? Are you Della's friend?"

"yes, Aunty! Do you mind if I can play with her in the garden; if she's ready by now"

"yes sure, she was getting a little bored too, you both can play in the garden. Careful don't go too far. The traffic's going to start soon"

"okay, aunty! Thank you!"

Della came outside. And I and daisy played with her.

"hi Della, good morning!"

"Hi, Jim! Good morning! You ready for school?"
"yep, a bit early. I was feeling a little bored, thought to play with you."
"yes, I was bored too. In which school are you going to study?
"me? Probably brookside elementary school."
"Hey! That's where I study!"
"Really? What a coincidence!"
Oh! I and Della are in the same school it's so much fun! I am in eighth and she's too! We are classmates!

# Chapter 5

"Jim! It has been so long since I have been looking for you!" Uncle Jack said coming towards us.

"Uncle Jack! I and Della are classmates!"

"Really? What fun?! I think you both need a ride to school."

"school!? Has it started?"

"yes, Jim. Look at the time!"

"oh yes! Let's go. Della, you can come with us"

"what a great idea Jim. Hop on Della" uncle jack said.

I was scared for going to my new school after a long time. But now, I am comfortable. I got a friend to play with in the class. But still, I feel a bit sad I don't know why! I went home said bye to dad, mom and daisy. I…. don't want to leave them but I have to as mom said I can't stay in this house forever.

We laughed and played and enjoyed this exciting ride to school. I asked Della that how was the school like. I just now can't wait to see my new friends and school but I. am a bit sensitive…. Honestly very sensitive! I don't want to cry in the class because of my sensitivity! Okay Jim! Don't think too much everything's is fine!

As we went quite further, I could see my new school! It was big and fun. I was lost in it. we went out of the car; I hugged uncle Jack and went with Della to my new classroom.

I arrived. The teacher and the students were staring at me, my head was down and my hands were folded in front.

The teacher came and put her hands back at my shoulder.

"Dear students we got a new student in our class. His name is Jim. I hope that you all will help him and make him feel better in our class".

"Hi Jim! The students said.

I sat on my allotted seat and got a sudden shock behind me. It was a student at my back. big, fat and so hässlich!

He said "hey kid you are not going to stay happy for so long! Just wait till I punch your face!"

"hey Bob! You dare not say anything to Jim!" a boy besides me said.

"hey you! Harry stop teaching me what to do or I'll disfigure your face too!" bob said.

"you want me to complain to ma'am?" harry asked bob

"just wait till ma'am goes then I'll see you!" bob said frustratedly.

The boy turned towards me and said "Jim, don't worry bob's quite a bully. You just stay away from him. Hi! I'm Harry."

"hi! Harry thanks a lot for saving me."

"No problemo!"

So, the class started ma'am taught us science, SST, and my least favorite in which I'm a zero MATHS! Oh boy I am just so scared of this thing!

Fine, we had a games period too so in that there we had a football selection for a tournament. I enrolled my name and as I've told you I'm good in every sport, every subject and everything except math!

And…. I got selected! Yeah well, the best first day for me!

At the dispersal Uncle Jack came to pick me and Della up.

"how was your day champ?" Uncle Jack asked.

"The best day ever uncle Jack! I made a new friend his name is Harry and the best part; I got selected in our school's football team!"

"I suppose today was lucky for you! Are you happy now?"

"yes, uncle Jack!"

"did you met a bully in school?"

"yes, Uncle Jack. He's bob! I don't really like him!"

"you see, when I was of your age; there were many bullies in my school too."

"really? Uncle Jack. How did you handle them?" Della asked.

"I just stayed away from them most of the times but one thing Jim your mother's and my father told me was that 'we must never stay quiet when something bad is happening in front of us. Our action at that time will write our future'.

"well Uncle it's quiet not getting in my head but I'll do as you say" Both the children said confidently.

They arrived at home and uncle Jack stayed at Jim's home for a while. They had tea and Jim changed his sweaty clothes. Then they had some tea time talk and uncle Jack left Jim after kissing him on his forehead.

Jim shared each and every detail with his mother about his school and then he had slept as he was very tired. After a few hours of sleeping in his bed he played football outside with daisy and then he did his homework.

It was evening Jim's father had arrived home.

"dad!" Jim exclaimed.

"hello son! How was your day?" dad said hugging Jim.

"it was wonderful! I got selected in my school's football team!"

"well done! Come let's have our dinner!"

They had a nice lunch and Jim went to his bedroom.

When Jim was sleepy enough, he heard a voice! He woke up from his bed and looked out through the window. It could not be daisy because she was sleeping with Jim on his bed.

"what could it be?" he murmured.

As he went outside, he saw a forest very far from his house. He then looked closely he saw a white light shaking like the wind up and down. He tried to look more closely and he saw a woman with a disfigured face who had some blood marks on her face with cuts on her hand and shoulders! She stared at Jim strangely. She smiled and Jim could see her bloody and sharp teeth which looked so creepy. She bent her body at the right and flew in the sky. Jim! Jim's heartbeat was getting fast and fast as the evil was coming towards him! She came closer and closer. Her sharp nails were so deadly and those captured Jim's throat! He cried in fear!

# Chapter 6

Jim! Della cried. "what happened?"

Jim opened his eyes. There was nothing. He saw Della at the window of next door.

"Della didn't you see it?!"

"See what?"

"Nothing"

Jim saw that Della was having a telescope through which she was looking at the stars.

"nice telescope!"

"oh! Thanks! You want to see through it?"

Jim was silent for a moment he was thinking that whether he would go or not.

"thank you, Della, but....

"but what?"


"Okay, I'm coming"

Jim went into Della's house and into her room. Della was looking at the planets. As Jim loves space he looked into it excitedly.

He whooped "wow! It's so beautiful! Wait! Is that Saturn?!"

"yep! I love looking in space. especially when I feel; tensed."

"so do I! Wait, is there any problem?

"No," she sighed.

"I can help!"

"Actually, Jim. I miss my mom. She went for some work and she's very late. She's also not answering my call."

"Oh, don't worry. She'll come back! probably she's busy. Okay, Let's not talk about your mom. it will make you miss her more."

" I hope so! right"

Della, can I ask you something?"

"Sure, what is it?"

"Della I saw something there in that forest; something paranormal. do you know anything about it?"

Della stayed silent and a bit tensed for a moment.

"if you don't want to answer it's fine! Sorry"

"no problem, Jim, I will tell you. This story is spread all over the town. You know, once there was a woman named Maria. Her car broke in between that forest. There was no internet so she couldn't place a call. She got hesitated and she was all alone in the growing dark. Suddenly, someone came towards her with a knife in his/ her hands and murdered that woman. After that, no one crosses that road. Whosoever does so never comes back. Many people have seen that woman with a doll."

"Really? But why does she capture me?"

"I don't know Jim. I'm really scared. Probably she has something to do with you."

"Della, I don't believe in these stories they are all fake! And if it's true I'll check by myself. Probably I've been dreaming and sleepwalking!"

"but Jim….

"but, what, nothing Della! I got to go. Good Night! And; thank you for letting me use your telescope it was fun."

Jim said stopping Della's words in between.
"good night! Jim. Sleep well!" Della said with a sigh.

"was Della saying the truth? Is that woman have something to do with me? What if she wants to kill me? Was that a dream?" all these kinds of questions were circling in my head. If I honestly say I feel a bit insecure. I hugged Daisy tightly and slept.

# Chapter 7

"what am I doing here? I was at home." Jim said by seeing himself lay on a grass in a lonely forest.

the darkness surrounded everything except there was a little light coming which gave a little hope to Jim somehow. The light was like a fire. Jim walked towards the light which grew bigger and bigger by the time he went forward.

When Jim reached very close to the light, he saw an old man sitting over a half-cut tree wood.

"hello, child what are you doing here at this time?"

"I don't know sir; I was in my bedroom and now I'm suddenly arrived here!"

"sit here my child. Haven't you heard about the woman who haunts everyone here? You should go back your home, before she captures you"

"I'm sorry sir but I don't believe in these kind of norms"

The old man after hearing this put his head down and then Jim heard some strange voices like someone screaming.

"are you okay sir..." Jim said stammering.

The old man held his head forward and his eyes were all white! He came closer to Jim. Closer and closer and he said in a horror voice!

"you don't believe in it! she's right behind you!!"

Jim could hear his heartbeat he looked behind apprehensively and no one was there! he moved his head down to the old man and…. he was not there!

Jim turned back and the same woman in the white dress was besides him and she cried "you are going to die! And laughed evilly.

Jim cried very loudly!

"Jim what happened?!" mom came running towards Jim's bedroom.

"she will kill me! Jim said shouting again and again.

"what happened Jim! Tell me!"

Jim was out of control. He was feeling that the whole world is broken into pieces and he's the last one to be alive along with that woman.

The woman was besides Jim's bedroom and smiling. Jim was petrified.

Jim hugged mom and asked if mom could sleep with him today. Daisy was barking at the place where the woman was standing. Mother stopped the dog.

"Jim it must have been a bad dream. Don't worry I'm here" mom said.

Somehow, that night I slept but the woman was still running in my head. I have to do something about it.

# Chapter 8

The next day, Jim didn't went to school. Della was sure that something bad has happened. She made a visit to Jim's home after coming back from school.

Knock- knock the door sounded.

"come in" said Jim in a tired manner

"it's me, Jim. Something has happened. Please tell me about it. what has happened?"

Jim was sitting on his couch near the window with his hands closed and he in a strained manner.

"Della, I don't want to make you troubled"

"you never make me trouble! Unless you don't tell me, what has happened; I am not going to leave this room. Please tell me."

"Della, now I am believing in ghosts. I saw that woman last night. When I woke, I saw myself in a forest and that woman was there. I also saw her in my bedroom last night."

Della put her hands on Jim's shoulder. "Jim, I told you. That woman surely has something to do with you!"

"how do I get out of it Della?! That woman seems like to latch herself on me"

"don't give up Jim there would definitely be a way in which we can finish her"

"you are right Della. I won't give up! I'll go to that woman by myself! I'll ask her what she wants from me!" said Jim looking sanguinely at Della.

"but Jim it's very dangerous! She has already troubled you a lot!"

"I know Della but I won't waste my life like this. I have to speak up for myself. I go and see her tomorrow only. You just do me a favor by telling me the road where she lives"

"no, Jim I'll be going with you"

"No Della! It's too risky. You stay here. She has something to do with me not you!"

"but Jim I'm your friend and I will never leave a friend behind!"

"but Della......

"But, what nothing Jim! I'm going and it's final"

Jim was speechless so he didn't say anything. now he and Della have to get ready for the most adventurous andriskiest journey ever!

# Chapter 9

The next day started and Jim and Della were ready to fight the ghost. It was early at almost 5 AM. Mom was sleeping in her bed. Jim went towards her.

"mom I'm sorry; but I have to go. I know you would stop me. But I…. can't live like this and risk your life with me too! I'll miss you. I hope I see you again. Jim probably for the last time hold his mother's hand, kissed her on her forehead and went.

Jim sat on his bicycle and Daisy was back at him. Glared at him strangely.

"Daisy it's too risky! You go back I can't take you along with me!"

But Daisy was too loyal that she didn't move from there. Jim having no choice had to insist to Daisy and dropped her in the house and locked the front door. So, she wouldn't come out. The way to open the door above was too high for Daisy.

Jim packed everything he might be needing in a small bag and went towards the forest. He didn't wait for Della to come too. But he don't know that she was there following him.

Jim reached the forest but he didn't know the road on which the ghost is. After all he is new and was only able to know the path to the forest and that also from the internet. Suddenly, Jim heard a noise. It was like the shaking of the grass. He got back and looked there; it was Della.

"Della go back home! I'm serious!"

"And I'm serious too! I am not going back!"

"Why are you so persistent?!" Jim asked angrily.

"oh! I'm persistent? You are! Now come on, Jim. One is always better than two! Now let me tell you the way where that horror woman is. Come on!"

Della already left and Jim followed her. They went a few kilometers and roamed and roamed. At last, they arrived at a bridge.

Jim stopped still for a second.

"Jim what happened?"

It was the same bridge that Jim found when he was arriving at Newbrook in his dream.

"Della it's not capable to hold our cycle's weight too! We need to walk!"

"I'm fine with walking."

They left their cycles aside and hopped in. the bridge was too old and narrow. It was almost like you are waking on a rope. They took teeny-tiny steps to make sure they didn't fall. Della reached at first.

Poor Jim afraid of heights. Went slowly I bet more slower than a tortoise! Holding the rope.

"hey! Jim, are you scared? Need any help?"

"can't you see? I'm scared…. And then this bridge…. I'm gonna fall!"

"hold on I gotcha!"

Della, fearlessly went and helped Jim cross that bridge. They both completed their first level and went further.

After walking a few miles; Jim was hungry.

"Dell' you want to eat something?"

"yep! For sure I'm hungry!"

Jim's safety bag had some food and water in it they took a break sitting in the shade of a tree and had talks.

"Jim, I hear something"

"what is it?'

"It's like someone walking. Heading towards us!"

"Della go behind that tree and hide! And give me my safety bag!"

They heard someone whistling! Who do you think it could be?

That thing when reached close to the tree; Jim took a small wooden rod and with his full strength attacked the thing.

"What?!"

# Chapter 10

"HARRY?!!" they both shouted. What are you doing here?!"

"ouch! You just killed me dude!" harry said rubbing his head.

"you see, I was taking a little morning cycle round around the road when I though to try I different route. I reached at your neighborhood and found you both. I thought to say hi; but you were in hurry. So, I followed you! And now I'm here!"

"Oh- Ho!" said Jim and Della slapping their Foreheads.

"Harry, I think you should go back." suggested Jim.

"yes, Jim's right Harry! You should go back."

"No- No, now I'm here and now I'm not going back at any cost. And firstly, what are you doing here? And I don't think it's too risky being here. You are not catching the ghost who lives here. are you?"

"if we say we are?"

"means. You really catching that ghost!"

"yes, now… do you want to stay here?"

"I……… would…. LOVE TO!!"

"huh!"

"I really wanted to catch a ghost! Let's go!"

"oh! Della, I don't think now he's going to go back!"

"Yes, Jim we have to take him with us." They both sighed.

"okay you can come Harry. Go ahead."

And now Harry, Jim and Della the three were in the adventure to fight the ghost and solve the mystery about 'the road that never ends'.

"can I ask you something?"

"tell Harry"

"why do you want to catch the ghost"

"we'll tell you later…"

"okay, well I'm so excited!"

As they went further, Jim stepped on something. It's a note. Which says

**"it's still time, you can go back kids or**

**You all will die!"**

**From- the ghost of the 'road that never ends'**

"hey guys I've got a note."

"see, Jim. We'll show that ghost that neither we are scared, nor we are going to die. She's the one who's on the last moments of her life" Della said.

"but Della, she's a ghost"

"yes, Harry she's a ghost. So what?"

"actually, you said 'life' and she's already dead! She is not alive!"

"whatever Harry!" Della said in an annoyed tone.

As they kept walking, the sun began to set.

"I think we better prepare for the night"

"Yes, Jim let's do it. Harry, can you collect some woods to light the fire with me?"

"yeah, sure"

"I am preparing for the bed. I think we can use that hollow tree it has a big hole under it. I can use leaves to make them some cushiony…. for Harry"

"what do you mean for Harry? Where you both are going to sleep?" harry asked.

"well, harry I got just one tent in my safety bag, only two people can fit."

"okay!"

# Chapter 11

Della and Harry lighted up the campfire and Jim heated some food left with him on it. moreover, he also made the tent with the help of his fellow friends and made the…. Leaves bed for; Harry.

They ate their dinner and slept in their places. Jim was not feeling sleepy he went outside to observe the stars.

"They are so beautiful!" he whooped

"yes, very beautiful, isn't it?"

"Della you should be asleep by now."

"Are you asleep? Not feeling sleepy right?"

"yes, I miss my mom."

"yeah, I can see that," Della said sitting next to him.

" oh! yes. Have your mom come back yet?"

" Probably now she will be at home."

" I hope so, Della."

"How come are you so sensitive Jim?"

"I don't know…"

"Della, …

"yes?"

"I want to thank you Road helping me. I never expected a friend to be so protective. Especially with whom I just met."

"Well, I found you nice. You see, the way the person talks; gives us a clue about what how he/ she is like. You like helping others and you are also a bit shy but you are probably the best person I've ever met."

"thank you, Della!" he said smiling and glaring into Della's eyes. His eyes were shining brightly like the bliss of a comet rain that fills the sky with light at night. They both were happy and forgot all the problems they have been through by just talking on this chilly night. It felt like they both met the persons they would love all their life and.........

BOOM!

"Ah! HARRY! Can't you give us some spare time!?"

"oh, sorry Della, I was having a very nice dream. I was hitting that fatty bob!"

Ah! Said both slapping their foreheads.

"Della, I think we should sleep by now. we have to wake up early. Let's go back in the tent"

"Yes, you're right!"

All the children finally slept well and woke up early in the morning. You all are thinking that how did they wake up so early? Let me tell you!

BEEP-BEEP!!!

AH! What is that strange and loud noise!?

"Oh sorry, you both. It's my watch. It has been set early in the morning" said Harry trying to off the alarm.

"why it is so loud?!"

"well because Jim, I don't know! We just woke early that benefit" Harry said.

"Okay! Jim, Harry, let's start our route! We will reach our destination by evening and that's the right time when she'll come out.

The children again started their route. They went down the woods and stopped by a river.

"let's wait here and have some rest" Jim suggested.

They sat near the rocks and put their legs under the water. Jim got still for a moment.

"What happened dude?" Harry asked.

"I'm feeling something. Something bad going to happen"

"How are you so sure?"

"I can feel it. she's here."

"Jim stop scaring me! Della, he's lying, isn't he?"

"I don't think so"

And the thing that happened was jaw-dropping. The clouds covered the sky and Jim was flying! His eyes got red and his nerves became visible! He is groaning and a monster-like voice said.

"You both are so fools! I'm not the real Jim.

"what? Then where's the real one?!"

"children I warned you earlier. But you didn't run out of the forest and now that you are so close to reaching my place, I won't let you do it. Jim's with me. I've hidden him in a secret place where you'll never find him. It's still time to escape the forest!" the woman laughed evilly and disappeared.

# Chapter 12

"Harry what are we going to do? We can't leave Jim!"

"so, are you telling me we are going to fight that witch?!"

"yes, we have to save Jim."

"Della, I think I am going to die!... Oh, I remember I got some work to do I'll be back...."

"Harry!!"

"Yes!"

"you are coming with me! Alright?"

"as you say, Della" Harry said with a sigh.

They went to the witch's place which was just a few miles away. At evening, as they calculated they reached the place. It was foggy everywhere.

"I can't neither see the witch nor Jim." Harry said

"we need to find. This is definitely the road that never ends"

"Della, can you see it?"

"what?"

"see there's a lantern there and its.... Lighting. Probably the witch has left it for us."

"yes, let's check out."

They hold the lantern and it pretty much helped them to fill some lightning. It was the time. The sunset. and the darkness filled the sky. Della and Harry were able to see only the lantern's light and the fog which surrounded the place.

They decided to walk. They walked and walked and walked. But the road didn't end. As the name says 'the road never ends'

"Oh, Della! I'm exhausted! What the hell this road isn't finishing?!

"I don't know. Hmm… look! There's a hut over there. let's check it out. Probably Jim's there?'

"Della, I think…… that's a haunted house!"

"Shut up! Harry. Come on don't be a scaredy cat!"

"okay I'm coming."

They went inside the house. It looked like it was really old. It was filled with disgusting things! Yack! Can you believe it?! spider webs on the hut, fingers, eyeballs, and a…. what is that? a human heart!? Inside a bottle?!

Gross!!

"Della I am feeling nauseated! Can we go back? this is surely a witch's house who do black magic! She will kill me! I'm going!"

"wait! Harry, I found a note! It's something like a riddle."

"Can we go out then read it please…!"

"okay!"

They went out and Della opened the note and read it aloud.

**'there's a big tree, under the forest; which holds a mystery,**

**Find the truth to free him, if you want to save Jim.'**

**Unknown**

"we don't even know who he belongs to. How are we going to find Jim?"

"I don't know Della. But let's follow the note."

They keep repeating the message until they found a clue and went on the road.

They kept walking and found the big tree. The tree was hollow. They looked in the hole and found a doll.

"Della…. Is it what I'm thinking… A HORROR DOLL!? I am very much afraid of this. I'm going!"

Poor Harry. Tried to escape but Della captured him again…

"Harry, we are very close. I saw a photo of a witch with the same doll in the hut we have to go back!"

# Chapter 13

They went back to the hut and found the photo. They got the first answer. This means that the doll that the witch had has been used in some kind of practice of black magic for sure. Probably the witch wanted to do black magic on someone. The witch may be the ghost too. She must have found out that the three friends would come here and probably will find a way to….

"Jim!" Della cried as she saw Jim fainted at a corner of the hut.

"Wake up buddy!" Harry cried

"wake up Jim.! Why isn't he not waking up Harry?!"

"I know!"

Harry took out his shoe and probably you all have guessed what he did to wake Jim up?

Oh, Jim finally woke up because of Harry's _________ (yes! Fill the dash…SOCKS!)

"Oh! Jim I am so glad you woke up!" Della said hugging him.

"yes, I'm fine but what you both are doing here?"

"we came here to save you." Harry said.

"Oh, thank you guys! You are the best friends ever!"

Well for sure, 'a friend in need is a friend indeed'

"when the witch captured you?" Della asked.

"when I was sleeping. I saw her but she made me smell something and I got fainted. she brought me here and I asked her what she did with me. So, she said that she has got to know that we three will kill her and that's why she wants us to leave."

"Is she that witch?" Harry asked pointing his finger on the portrait.

"No, she was someone in a white dress with a locket."

"a locket?" Della asked strangely.

"yes, a brown locket."

Della got freeze for a moment.

"something wrong Dell'?"

"No, I'm fine."

Then Della and Harry told everything about the things that they saw.

"okay we know the truth and we are going to kill her." Jim said.

They went to find the witch. Half an hour passed and they found her sitting on a bench. The bench was at the opposite side. Her back was visible.

"you have come here?" she asked

"yes, and today is your last day." Harry said he continued "oh, I spoke such a heroic dialogue!"

She stood up from the bench and walked. Her black hair covered her face and her white gown was gliding through the wind. The moon became visible as it came out of the black clouds. She slowly turned her head towards them. the body of her was like cramping. She turned her head a bit right side and looked strangely her big nails were red. She walked towards them.

She used her powers and made Jim and Harry fly and suffocating their necks.

Della looked tensely at the woman. Looked like she knows that woman. After much wait she said.

"stop it, Mom!" Della cried

Jim and Harry fell.

"MOM!?" they said.

"yes, she's, my mom! I recognize her face and that locket. it's her!"

The woman turned to be like a human again and hugged Della.

"Oh, Della, I missed you!"

"Mom, what happened? Where did you go?" Della asked crying.

"dear, that witch did her black magic on me when I was crossing this road in my car at night. She said that she wants me to kill you. When I denied she took me under her control and hypnotized me to be the ghost of this road."

"Mom, then what about the rumor about this road? is the story fake?"

"Della, the incident of murder happened with the witch's daughter and she wanted to take revenge from the people who killed her daughter. She killed the convicts but as this rumor spread all over the town, she chose me to be the ghost."

"Mom, you don't worry. We'll kill her and free you!"

"Yes aunty. You don't worry. We'll handle it." Jim said.

"But it's very dangerous. You won't be able to do it!"

"don't worry aunty we got her weakness her beloved doll!" harry replied.

"You got her? I wrote the message so that you can find it. I was prohibited to go near that doll if we destroy it the witch's power will be finished!"

"Okay let's finish her!" all the children said.

But who knows, the witch came there.

"children I told you! To get out. Now I'll not leave you!" she groaned.

"this is the woman I saw" Jim cried

"What you children think that this ghost will help you? I have hypnotized her she'll obey me!"

"She's not a ghost! you are!" Della cried.

"Hey old woman look here what we got! Your weakness...!" harry said in a cheerful manner.

"No! please give that doll to me!" she cried.

Jim took the doll and destroyed her by crunching her under his foot.

"NO!!" the witch cried in pain. At last, she vanished and Della's mom became free.

They all hugged each other and the road became a normal road again and now it was safe. All thanks to Jim, Della and Harry who made it possible. Also, to Della's mom! Without her message it was nearly impossible to defeat the witch.

Their normal life started again. Della and her mom lived happily. Jim and Della became more close friends and Harry? He still the same! But more experienced than he was before.